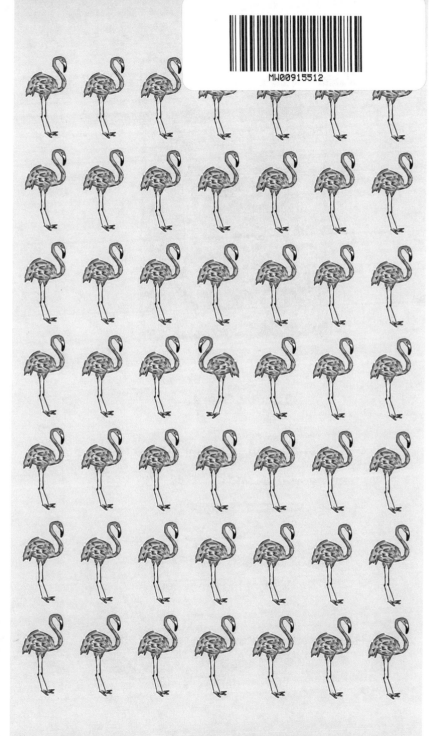

Thomas George...

...is an author who, like Hans-Peter the flamingo, once lived by a cold river, in a grey town, on a green island.

Similarly, he likes fish, seagulls, and looking at his reflection.

However, he has no strong feelings about ducks.

Sandra Unterkircher...

...is a designer who largely compensates for the author's inability to draw straight lines.

As an Austrian, she finds it difficult to conceptualise the sea at all.

Despite this, she draws an excellent flamingo.

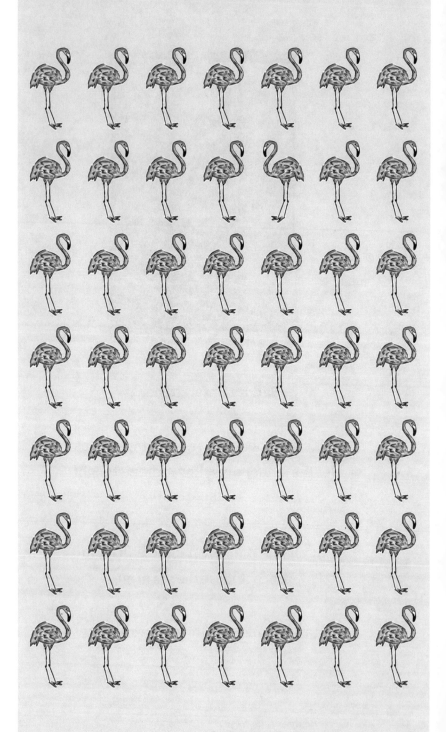

A Very Special Flamingo

Thomas George
with Sandra Unterkircher

A Note on Flamingos

by Thomas George

I like to think that flamingos are pink because... well, they can be. It's as a good a reason as any to be wonderful.

People, like flamingos, don't need a reason to be different.

However, anything that finds itself in the wrong place can seem threatening. Particularly to people who are lonely and scared.

Sometimes, this means that the flamingos with the brightest feathers feel the need to change – and it makes the world around us all the less interesting when they do.

This story is as much about finding yourself in a place that isn't perfect as it is about finding a perfect place.

Whether you've got pink feathers or grey ones... I hope this story helps you find the flamingo inside.

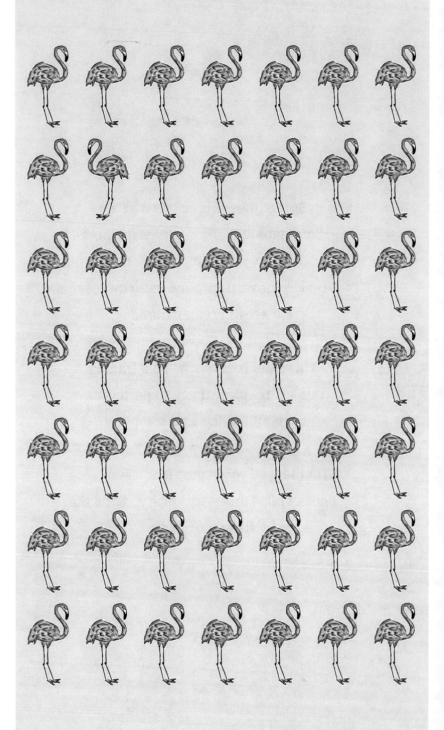

Chapter One

Hans-Peter, Flamingo of a Town

On a cold river, in a grey town, on a green island, lived a very special, very pink flamingo.

Although he was a river flamingo, this river was not his home.

Hans-Peter, the flamingo, was a very special, very handsome flamingo indeed.

So handsome that he often stood in the deepest water to be closer to his beautiful reflection.

He knew that he was the only flamingo on the cold river, in the grey town, and perhaps on the whole green island.

Hans-Peter thought this made him very special. There were no others like him for miles around.

Beautiful and interesting as he was, Hans-Peter was confused. This was because no one else seemed to think he was special.

Often, he spread his great pink wings and told stories of his home in the beautiful, far-off land with its wonderful creatures.

Yet the ducks on the cold river were not impressed. They did not think that being very pink – or even coming from a far-off place – made anyone special.

Instead, the ducks simply ignored Hans-Peter, then swam along.

Hans-Peter could not understand ducks at all. He did not know why they did so little, but quacked so much.

They quacked about nests, about bread, and then about nests and about bread again.

Sometimes, this quacking lasted the whole night long.

The only thing they did not quack about was what a special flamingo Hans-Peter was.

Bread was okay, and a nest would be nice. But bread was not as good as the tasty pink shrimps Hans-Peter had eaten in his home far away. Nor would a nest on the cold river be as comfortable as a nest in the far-off land.

Hans-Peter dreamt of returning home, a place where such a very special flamingo could belong. Yet he did not know the way. He was stuck on the grey island.

Hans-Peter thought that someone in the town might find him special, even if the ducks did not. With this in mind, he left the river to explore.

Things were not much better in the grey
town.

Hans-Peter thought that the children
there might find him special. However,
they did not seem to like him very much.

Hans-Peter did not like the children
very much either. They were even less
interesting than the ducks.

They could not swim, they could not fly,
and they ate disgusting food.

As he was hungry, Hans-Peter had to eat some human food too.

The fish in tins was too salty, and it reminded Hans-Peter of the roaring sea far away...

... and as a river flamingo, Hans-Peter did not like the sea at all.

The grey pigeons of the grey town could fly, but they were even less friendly than the children.

The pigeons definitely did not think that Hans-Peter was special. They flapped, shouted, and cooed nasty words.

Hans-Peter did not understand. He thought he was far more special than the pigeons and the children. Yet the pigeons and the children had more food, more friends, and seemed to be happier in every way.

Why, thought Hans-Peter, could nobody see that he was a very special flamingo?

That night, Hans-Peter returned to his favorite spot in the river to look at his beautiful reflection.

In the moonlight, he could see that he was no longer as special and as magnificent as he once was.

The terrible salty fish had made his feathers slightly grey, while the grey town had made his eyes sad and dull.

He looked at his reflection until the morning came.

Surely, he thought, there was somewhere that others would see what a special flamingo he was.

Feeling determined, Hans-Peter smoothed his feathers and left the cold river, in the grey town, to explore the rest of the green island.

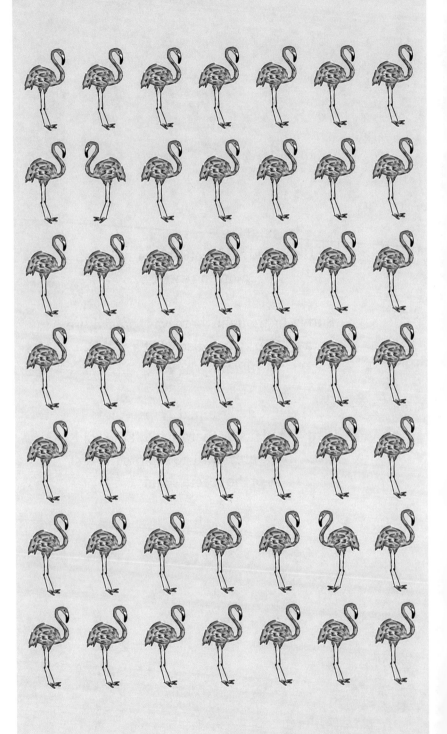

Chapter Two
Hans-Peter, Flamingo of an Island

Hans-Peter loved to fly. He felt free
and happy to be alone, away from the
greyness of the town.

Yet, when he landed in the dark forest,
his sadness returned. Again, he felt too
special for this place.

In the dark forest, his pink feathers were
too bright for the angry owls, who chased
him away...

...to the snowy mountains.

There, it was too cold to think of anything but building a nest to stay warm, like the silent eagles all around him.

Yet Hans-Peter was not an eagle any more than he was a duck. In fact, he thought that he was much more special than either.

He did not want a nest in such a cold place, and he did not want to stay with birds who did. He shivered, and headed back to the sky...

...before landing on a golden, sandy
beach by the roaring sea.

At the beach, the birds were much more
pleasant than those on the cold river, or
in the grey town, or in the dark forest, or
on the snowy mountain.

The friendly seagulls knew a lot about
the roaring sea. Although Hans-Peter did
not like the sea, their friendliness helped
him feel better about it.

The friendly seagulls listened to Hans-Peter's stories of the far-off land, with its wonderful creatures and splendid colours.

They told their own tales of giant squid and human boats, which took bright-pink shrimps across a sea that had no end.

Hans-Peter did not know if the stories were true, but he did not think it mattered too much.

Hans-Peter stayed on the golden, sandy beach for many days. He talked often to the friendly seagulls, but he stayed mostly in the shade, a long way from the water.

He did not go to the shore to cool down, or even to look at his beautiful reflection. Although it was very interesting to look at, the salty sea made Hans-Peter scared.

It was not just the salt, which made his feathers grey. It was that the sea was so big, he could not see to the other side.

One afternoon, Hans-Peter stood on one leg next to his best seagull friend, Doris. They looked together over the endless, roaring sea.

"What's over there?" he asked.

"I don't know," squawked Doris.

"Sometimes it's okay not to know."

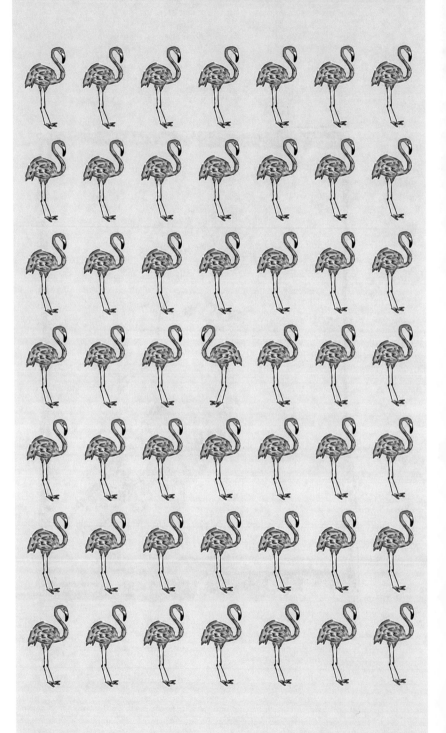

Chapter Three
Hans-Peter, Flamingo of the Sea

Hans-Peter thought about what Doris had said for a while. He decided that he liked Doris very much.

But Hans-Peter was not a seagull, any more than he was an eagle or a duck. He had to go to the only place where people would see how special he was. He had to go home to the far-off land.

So, he spread his wings once more and flew, and flew, and flew.

Hans-Peter had never flown so far, or so high, or so fast. He was becoming tired and wanted to get out of the sky.

It was not just because he was hungry. He wanted to find his way home to the far-off land, with its wonderful creatures, and make a nest.

There, he could be warm and happy, and others would see what a very special flamingo he was.

Hans-Peter did not know exactly where he was going, only that it felt like he was flying in the right direction.

Yet the roaring sea was so big.

As the freezing wind blew through his pink feathers, he began to think that the salty water below really did have no end.

The bitter wind reminded Hans-Peter of
the cold river in the grey town.

This reminded him of the ducks who did
so little but quacked so much. The ducks
who did not think he was special.

Perhaps they had been right. Perhaps
Hans-Peter was not a very special
flamingo after all, but a very foolish one.

Feeling sad and lonely, Hans-Peter
drifted off to sleep...

...and fell down and down into the salty sea below.

In his sleep, Hans-Peter felt the salty sea
bring him safely to the shore.

When he awoke, his bill was full of
terrible, salty water, and his pink
feathers were heavy with wet, muddy
sand.

He stood up, shook himself down, and
looked up.

Then he saw the most beautiful sight he
had ever seen.

Endless flamingos: tall, handsome, and more colorful than any birds he had ever seen, were spread in an ocean of pink in front of him.

They stood closely together and sang beautiful songs of the sea.

Hans-Peter was lost.

As he explored, he realised that the sea had not brought him home. This was somewhere he had never been before.

It did not seem like a good place for flamingos to live at all.

It was still very cold. Worse still, the sea air was heavy with the taste of salt, the type that made his feathers grey.

Hans-Peter looked once more at the beautiful pink birds. Clearly, these were sea flamingos.

This is why they could live by the salty water and stay bright, pink and wonderful.

It was not just their feathers.

As he walked through the crowds of beautiful birds, he could see that their eyes were not sad like his. They shone with peace, joy, and love.

Hans-Peter knew that he could never be a real sea flamingo, any more than he could be a duck, a pigeon, an owl, an eagle, or a seagull.

His curved bill was too short to eat the huge sea shrimps, and he would never like the salt of the roaring sea.

But when he looked at his reflection again, Hans-Peter decided that he liked being grey.

As the only grey flamingo on this new flamingo island, the others thought that this made him very special too.

His feathers would never return to being pink. Instead, he would stay a grey flamingo forever.

Although he liked his new feathers, it was the roaring sea, which he had once disliked so much, that reminded him him most that he was happy.

It was because the sea reminded Hans-Peter that he could be happy anywhere.

It did not matter whether he was a sea flamingo or a river flamingo. What mattered was being seen for who he really was – and seeing that in himself as well.

With this in his mind, Hans-Peter found
the quietest corner of the beach, where
the shady, fruit-filled trees grew.

He found some big, soft leaves, made a
nest, and lay down to sleep.

He felt, again, like a very special
flamingo.

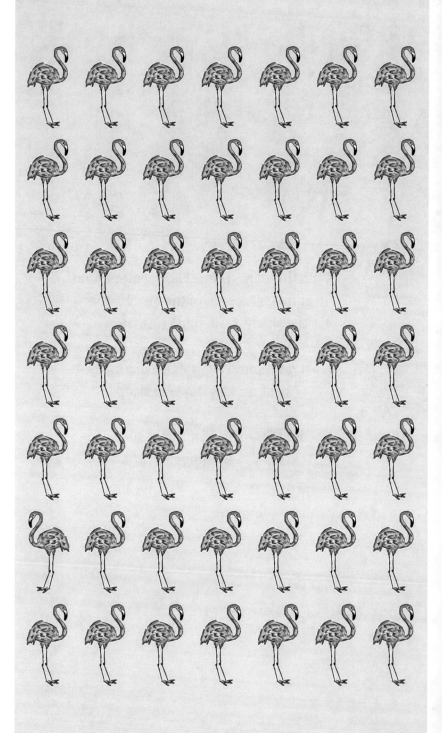

The End

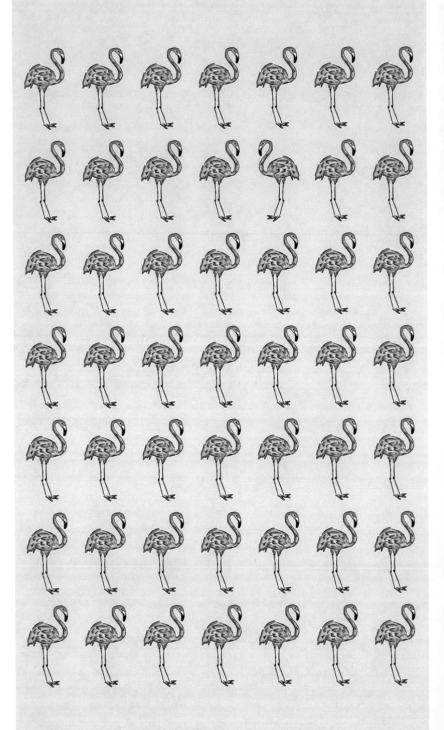

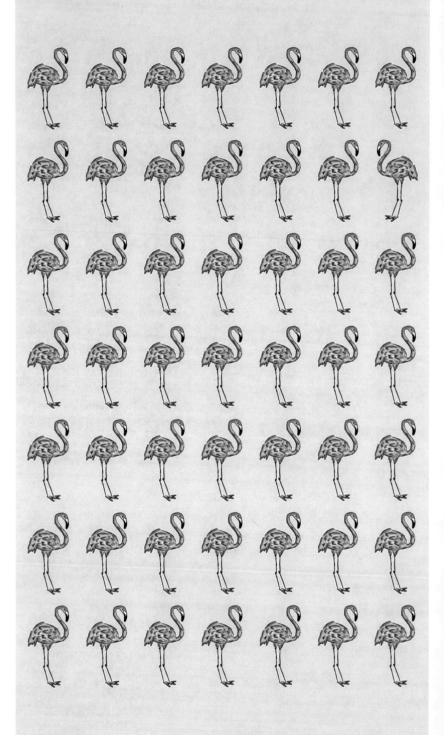

Made in the USA
Columbia, SC
24 November 2024

47445402R00043